Stories and rhymes in this book

HELLO, BEARS!

BIG BAD MUM'S WASH DAY

THE BIG BAD BEARS' SONG

NOISY BEARS

BEAR WEAR

BIG BAD GRANNY'S MOTORBIKE

ONE, TWO, THREE, FOUR, FIVE BEARS

NICE AND CLEAN

BE A BIG BAD BEAR!

Published by Ladybird Books Ltd
27 Wrights Lane London W8 5TZ
A Penguin Company
© LADYBIRD BOOKS LTD MCMXCIX
Produced for Ladybird Books Ltd by Nicola Baxter and Amanda Hawkes
The moral rights of the author/illustrator have been asserted

The Big Bad Bears

by Stephanie Barton
illustrated by Fran Jordan

Ladybird

BIG BAD MUM'S WASH DAY

Big Bad Mum had a brand new rumbly jumbly washing machine.

But she was too busy to read the instructions.

There was an awful lot of washing to be done. She put in...

Big Brother Bill's long smelly socks...

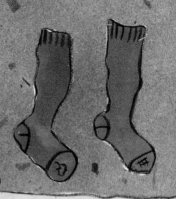

her own big stripey sweater...

Big Bad Granny's extra-long elegant dancing tights...

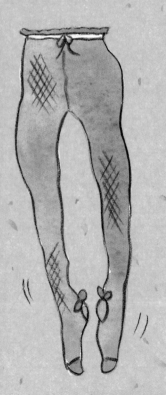

five pairs of Little Brother Pete's little-sized trousers...

...and Big Bad Dad's HUGE baggy pants.

Rumble jumble... the washing machine got to work.

And Big Bad Mum had time for a cup of Best Bear brew...

before she carried the washing out to the line.

But things didn't look
quite right.

Big Brother Bill's socks were not quite so LONG...

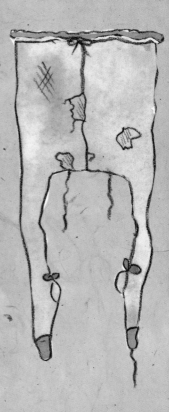

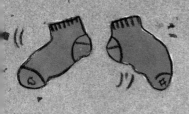

Big Bad Mum's sweater wasn't quite so BIG...

Big Bad Granny's tights were not quite so ELEGANT...

Big Bad Dad's pants were not quite so HUGE...

and Little Brother Pete's trousers didn't look quite so LITTLE-SIZED...

They were BIG and BAGGY
and could now fit every
Big Bad Bear except...

Little Brother Pete!

THE BIG BAD BEARS' SONG

We're gruff
and we're
grumpy.

We're BIG
and we're
BAD.

We're tough
and we're
jumpy,

So don't
make us
MAD!

NOISY BEARS

Big Brother Bill and
Little Brother Pete were
NOISY bears.

They were noisy
when they played
Bish Bash Bear
chasing.

"Stop that bishing and bashing," called Big Bad Mum...

but the Big Bad brothers didn't hear a word.

They were noisy when
they went Splish Splash
Bear swimming.

"Stop that splish-splashing,"
shouted Big Bad Dad,
but the Big Bad brothers
didn't hear a word.

They were noisy when they ate Bearghetti spaghetti.

"Stop that slurping!" said Big Bad Granny, but the Big Bad brothers didn't hear a word.

They were noisy when they
had a bath...

cleaned
their
teeth...

and
climbed into bed.

And then,
when Big Bad
Dad tucked
them in...

and Big Bad
Granny put
out the
light...

and Big Bad Mum gave
them each a big bear kiss...

those Big Bad Bear brothers fell fast asleep and were not noisy again until...

morning!

BEAR WEAR

Baggy pants,

Spotty pants,

Which ones shall I wear?

Stripey pants,

Dotty pants,

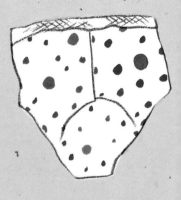

A bear just can't be bare!

BIG BAD GRANNY'S MOTORBIKE

Big Bad Granny drove
a Bearaway
Tearaway
Motorbike.

It had a shiny red sidecar
for passengers.

It was a motorbike
made to go fast...

and Big Bad Granny drove it
very fast indeed.

All the Big Bad Bears loved
Granny Bear's bike. It was
good for shopping.

It was good for
picnic trips.

It was good for going swimming.

And it was good for going to football matches.

But Big Bad Granny liked it best of all when, every Saturday night, she went to the Big Jig...

where she danced the
night away and never ever
came home until way past
Big Bad Bear bedtime!

ONE, TWO, THREE, FOUR, FIVE BEARS

One Big Bad Bear went shopping one day.

Two Big Bad Bears went out to play.

Three Big Bad Bears went for a ride.

Four Big Bad Bears stayed inside.

But five Big Bad Bears,
looking very fine...

Were all dressed up,
And going out to dine.

NICE AND CLEAN

"Let's do some painting,
Little Pete," said
Big Brother Bill.

Big Bad Mum
said, "Put on
your aprons...

and roll up
your sleeves.

Keep everything nice and clean, and DON'T get paint on the table!"

Then she went outside to practise her trampolining.

Big Brother Bill sat on his chair to paint. He painted a hill with a green train on it.

The green paint dripped down his arm and on to the chair.

Little Brother Pete kneeled up on his chair to paint. He painted a yellow car at a level crossing.

The yellow paint dripped down his arm and on to the chair.

Big Brother Bill went to look at Little Brother Pete's painting.

He sat down on Pete's chair.

Little Brother Pete went to look at Big Brother Bill's painting.

He sat down on Bill's chair.

Then they went to the window. "Mum!" they called. "Come and see! We've finished...

and we've kept everything nice and clean, and not a DROP on the table!"

BE A BIG BAD BEAR!

Stand on one leg like a Big Bad Bear!

Clap your hands like a Big Bad Bear!

Make a BIG noise like a Big Bad Bear.

Jump in the air! There! You're a Big Bad Bear!